Follow Mutzie's Journey—

Meet Mutzie

Amanda A. Parrish

Illustrations by Jason Fowler

the PeppertreePress

Sarasota, Florida

For information regarding permission, call 941-922-2662 or contact us at our website:
www.peppertreepublishing.com or write to:
the Peppertree Press, LLC.
Attention: Publisher
1269 First Street, Suite 7
Sarasota, Florida 34236

ISBN: 978-1-61493-599-5

Library of Congress Number: 2018908667

Printed September 2018

This book is dedicated to my wonderful husband for always believing in me

This is the story of a journey,
a search for a loving home,
and this story starts with a puppy
who felt very, very alone.

Within the walls of Pure Puppy Pet Shop lots of puppies lived.

In fact, there were oodles ...

beautiful bassets, dashing danes, lovely labs,

and perfect poodles.

Breathtaking breeds that could all win a prize...

...for being the perfect color, perfect shape, and perfect size.

Families would come day after day
and all would leave the exact same way,
with a proud new puppy and arms full of toys,
and happy, smiling, laughing little girls and boys.

There was one puppy though, that never went home,
and this was the puppy that felt so alone.
She lived in the back, in a cage on the right,
and this fuzzy pooch looked odd at first sight.

She wasn't a terrier. She wasn't a hound,
and Pure Puppy Pet Shop said she belonged at the pound.
Around her neck was a bandana of red
and Mutzie, her name, is what the cloth said.

With black and brown and gold wiry hair,
this mutt, named Mutzie, made everyone stare.

Her awkward long legs and floppy large ears
made her look different than her Pure Puppy peers.

Her shaggy tail was colored and long
and to say the least, she just didn't belong.

Day after day, she would watch families leave,

and day after day, it was hard to believe ...

that she would ever go home with a mom and a dad,

and this lonely thought made poor Mutzie sad.

One night when the pet shop was dark, and the puppies were down,

Mutzie lay awake with tears and a frown.

Tired of feeling odd and not loved as she was,

Mutzie's young mind was all abuzz.

She wanted to leave, get away from the store.
She thought to herself, There must be much more.

There must be a family who would choose to care
despite the fact I make everyone stare.

Just at that moment, as Mutzie lay there and cried,
a flash of light made her look outside.

A beautiful moon, in a crystal clear sky,
the magical light was a star shooting by.

Mutzie wagged her tail and jumped all around.
"Hooray, Hooray," an answer was found.

Mutzie closed her eyes and wished on that star,
wished that she could travel far ...

leave Pure Puppies and find a home,
a loving place to call her own.

Her eyes closed tight, her heart beating fast,
Mutzie heard her lock unclasp!

Her cage flew open and the front door unlocked.
Mutzie looked around, surprised and shocked.

This was it. Her wish had come true
and she knew, in an instant, what she had to do.

And though she was scared, this puppy named Mutzie,
she said to herself, "It's time to be gutsy."

So she took a step and walked out the front door,
and without another thought, ran away from that store.

Overcome with thrill, she ran straight out of town.
Her floppy ears flopping, she never slowed down.

She ran and ran, without looking back,
until all of a sudden she reached a train track.

She looked down the rail, heard the train whistle blow,
and in the distance saw the headlight aglow.

With all of her courage she got ready to jump,
and as the train passed by, she landed with a thump!

Aboard the train, away she flew.

Where she was going, she hadn't a clue.

But her journey had started, a new home she would find,

and she howled with joy as she left her old life behind!

CPSIA information can be obtained
at www.ICGtesting.com
Printed in the USA
BVHW020518051118
531719BV00001B/2/P